THE *Three Little Pigs*

Illustrated by **Ruth Bendel**

Published by

THE TOON STUDIO
O F   B E V E R L Y   H I L L S

THERE WAS once a mother pig who had three little pigs. This mother pig was very poor. She was so very poor that she could not keep her three little ones at home.
"You must go out into the world, little pigs, and seek your fortunes," the mother pig said one day.

So the three little pigs trotted out into the world.

The first little pig had not gone far when he met a man with a bundle of straw.

"Please, man, give me that straw to build a house," said he.

"I will," said the man. And he did, and the little pig built a house. Before long a wolf passed that way, knocked at the door of the little straw house, and called out: "Little pig, little pig, let me come in."

"No, no, by the hair of my chinny, chin, chin," answered the little pig. "Then I'll huff, and I'll puff, and I'll blow your house in," said the wolf. So he huffed, and he puffed, and he blew the house in. But the little pig had slipped away into the woods, so the wolf didn't make a dinner of him after all.

The second little pig met a man with a bundle of twigs. "Please, man, give me those twigs to build a house," said he.

"I will," said the man. And he did, and the little pig built a house.

Then along came the wolf, knocked at the door, and called out: "Little pig, little pig, let me come in."

"No, no, by the hair of my chinny, chin, chin," answered the little pig.

"Then I'll huff, and I'll puff, and I'll blow your house in," said the wolf.

So he huffed, and he puffed, and at last he blew the house in. But the second little pig had slipped out of the back door and hid in the thicket, so the wolf didn't make a dinner of him after all.

The third little pig met a man with a load of bricks.

"Please, man, give me those bricks to build a house," said he.

"I will," said the man. And he did, and the little pig built a house.

Then along came the wolf, knocked at the door, and called out: "Little pig, little pig, let me come in."

"No, no, by the hair of my chinny, chin, chin," answered the little pig.

"Then I'll huff, and I'll puff, and I'll blow your house in," said the wolf.

So he huffed and he puffed, and he puffed and he huffed, and he huffed and he puffed, and still he could not blow the house in. At last, when the wolf found out he could not blow the little house in, he gave it up and called out: "Little pig, little pig, I know where there is a nice field of turnips."

"Oh, do you? Where?" asked the little pig.

"In Mr. Smith's field. Would you like to come with me to get some?"

"Yes," said the little pig. "When?"
At six o'clock tomorrow morning."
The next morning the little pig got up at five
o'clock, went to Mr. Smith's field, and got the
turnips before the wolf came. At six o'clock
the wolf knocked at his door and called out:

"Are you ready, little pig?"
"Ready!" said the little pig. "I have been to
the turnip field and back again. My turnips
are now boiling in the pot."
The wolf felt very angry when he heard this,
but he made up his mind not to be beaten,

so he said, "Little pig, little pig, I know where there is a nice apple tree."
"Oh, do you? Where?" asked the little pig.
"In Mr. Brown's garden. Would you like to come with me to get some apples?"

"Yes," said the little pig. "When?"
"At five o'clock tomorrow morning."
The next morning the little pig got up at
four o'clock and went to Mr. Brown's
garden. No smoke rose from the chimney of
the little cottage. Very likely Mr. Brown was
asleep.

Even if he was not, there was a broad river between the house and the garden, and the little pig would have time to run away before Mr. Brown could cross the bridge.

The apple tree was on the bank of the river. The little pig climbed up and was eating

a ripe, rosy-cheeked apple when, lo and behold!
there was Mr. Wolf at the foot of the tree.
"Ah, ha! little pig, so you are here before me,"
said the wolf. "Are they not nice apples?"
"Yes, very," said the little pig, trembling.

"I will throw you down one. Here you are,"
and he threw down one. But he threw it so
that the apple fell on the green bank of the
river, far away from the tree.
Then it rolled and rolled, and the wolf had to

run a long way after it. While the wolf was racing to pick up the apple, quick as lightning the little pig climbed down. Then he ran for his life till he reached home safe and sound.

The next day the wolf came down again to the little pig's house and called out:
"Little pig, little pig, I know where there is a fair."
"Oh, do you? Where?" asked the little pig.
"At Shanklin. Would you like to come and go with me?"

"Yes," said the little pig. "When shall you be ready to go?"

"At three o'clock tomorrow morning."

So the next morning the little pig got up at two o'clock, went to the fair and bought a butter churn. On his way home what did he

see but the wolf coming up the hill! He was
in a great fright and did not know what to do.
So he jumped into the butter churn to hide.
But the butter churn turned round and did
not stay still. Round and round it turned as it
rolled down the hill with the pig in it. This
gave the wolf such a fright that he did not go
to the fair, but, after resting awhile, trotted
slowly home.

In the afternoon he went round to the little
pig's house, knocked, and called out:

"Little pig, little pig, I got a fright, I can tell you, as I went to the fair this morning. A big round thing rolled down the hill and nearly knocked me over. When it came rolling past me, I was too much afraid to look to see what it was."

"Ho, ho, ho, ho, ho!" laughed the little pig.
"Afraid, were you? Well, I can tell you all
about that. The big round thing that rolled
down the hill this morning was a butter churn
that I bought at the fair, and I was inside it."

Then the wolf was angrier than ever and called out: "Now little pig, I mean to eat you up, anyhow. I'm coming down the chimney."

"Oh, are you?" said the little pig, and as the wolf jumped down, the little pig took the lid off a large pot of boiling water that was on the fire. Down tumbled the wolf, right into the big bubbling pot. Then the little pig popped on the cover again.

So there was the end of the wolf, and the little pig lived happily ever afterward.